Pig and Horse
and the
Something Scary

Zoey Abbott

Abrams Books for Young Readers

New York

*For Mama, Veni, Al, Nako, Nobs, Oanh, Robyn, Subi,
Deirdre, Suz, Steiny, TJ, Sharmi, and loyal horses
everywhere. Special thanks to Dr. Veneta Stoyanova,
Dr. Michelle Bobowick, and SBA.*

The illustrations for this book were made with gouache, colored pencil, and sumi ink.

The quote *"Live in the sunshine, swim the sea, drink the wild air"* on page 20 is paraphrased from a line in Ralph Waldo Emerson's poem "Merlin's Song" (*Ralph Waldo Emerson: The Major Poetry*; Harvard University Press, 2015).

Cataloging-in-Publication Data has been applied for and may be obtained from the Library of Congress.

ISBN 978-1-4197-4501-0

Text and illustrations © 2022 Zoey Abbott
Book design by Jade Rector

Printed and bound in China
10 9 8 7 6 5 4 3 2 1

Abrams® is a registered trademark of Harry N. Abrams, Inc.

ABRAMS The Art of Books
195 Broadway, New York, NY 10007
abramsbooks.com

One morning, Pig woke up feeling a bit out of sorts.
So she decided to go over to Horse's house.

"I have something in my head, and it is scaring me," Pig said.

"What is it?" asked Horse.

"I can't say. I'm trying to ignore it."

"Perhaps if we take whatever-it-is for a bike ride in the sunshine,
 it will go away?" Horse offered.

"Maybe . . ."

"What a magnificent ride!"
exclaimed Horse.

"Quite lovely," answered Pig.

"But it's still there . . ."

"I have an idea! A dunk and splash.
Will a swim make it go away?" Horse wondered.

Pig thought it was worth a try.

"It's still there," Pig whispered.

"My word, still? Perhaps if we get you to laugh
really hard, it will go away?"
Horse thought this was her best idea yet.

"We look ridiculous, Pig!" Horse giggled.

"It's not funny, and besides, it's getting worse!"

Horse took Pig's hand. "You might just have to let whatever-it-is out."

"But I'm scared."

"Let's see . . . bike rides, swims, and
    silly hats don't seem to be working."

    "That is true. They are not working."

        Then Horse offered a serious plan.
        "Why don't we invite whatever-it-is to tea?"

        "I don't think you'll be able to handle it."

        "Of course I will, Pig. And besides, teatime
            brings out the best manners in everyone!"

So Pig and Horse set to work,
baking and making.

When the wobble jelly was set,

the chocolate cake cooled and iced,

the scones just right,

the watercress sandwiches sliced and arranged,

and the flowers meticulously chosen,

Horse said, "Are you ready?"

And Pig said, "If you are sure about this . . ."

Horse said she was sure.

Pig closed her eyes.

"What is that?" Horse trembled.

"It's the night. I'm afraid of the night!" Pig yelled out.

"Let's sing our favorite song!" cried Horse.

"*Live in the sunshine, swim the sea, drink the wild air.*"
They sang and sang and sang.

As the night ate more and more cake,
the night became smaller,

and smaller,

and smaller.

"There's more," Pig said.

This time it was sticky and thick like jam.

"What is it?" Horse asked.

"Sometimes, I'm scared of being alone!"

"I'm here," said Horse. "Take my hand."

The loneliness drank cupful after cupful of tea.

Pig and Horse held hands until the lonely jam melted away.

But there was still more . . .

"What is THAT?" Horse gasped.

"It's a story I read at bedtime last night!"

"That is a very scary story!"
Horse thought maybe they should run.

But there was only one thing to do:
Keep following the plan.

So Pig poured the last drops of tea for the storybook creature.

The creature inhaled it.

Pig offered wobble jelly, scones, and sandwiches.

The creature ate every last crumb.

And just as Pig worried she had nothing else to offer, she noticed the leftover night.

Then Pig remembered something about dogs.

This gave her an idea.

Just like that, Pig felt a great weight lift from her shoulders.

She felt the corners of her mouth lift, too.

Teatime had worked!

That evening, Pig and Horse made a double batch of pasta with cream sauce and grilled asparagus.

"How are you feeling now, Pig?" Horse asked.

"Much better now that I know that the night likes cake and a song.
Loneliness likes tea and a hand to hold. And whenever I want,
I can write my own ending for any storybook creature."

"You wrote a *really* good ending this time," Horse said with relief.

But then, just as they were sitting down to eat,

Pig thought she heard something in the garden. She decided to go have a look.

There was nothing there.

"Just in case," Pig said.

"We have more than enough,"
Horse agreed.